Chasing a Hat

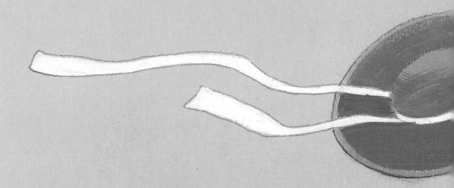

by Lilian Moore
pictures by Rosanne Litzinger

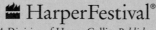

HarperFestival®
A Division of HarperCollinsPublishers

The wind
that whirled
your hat
away

furled a flag

filled a sail

raced a boat

tugged a kite
tweaked its tail

towed a cloud

rode a wave

shook a willow

bent a birch

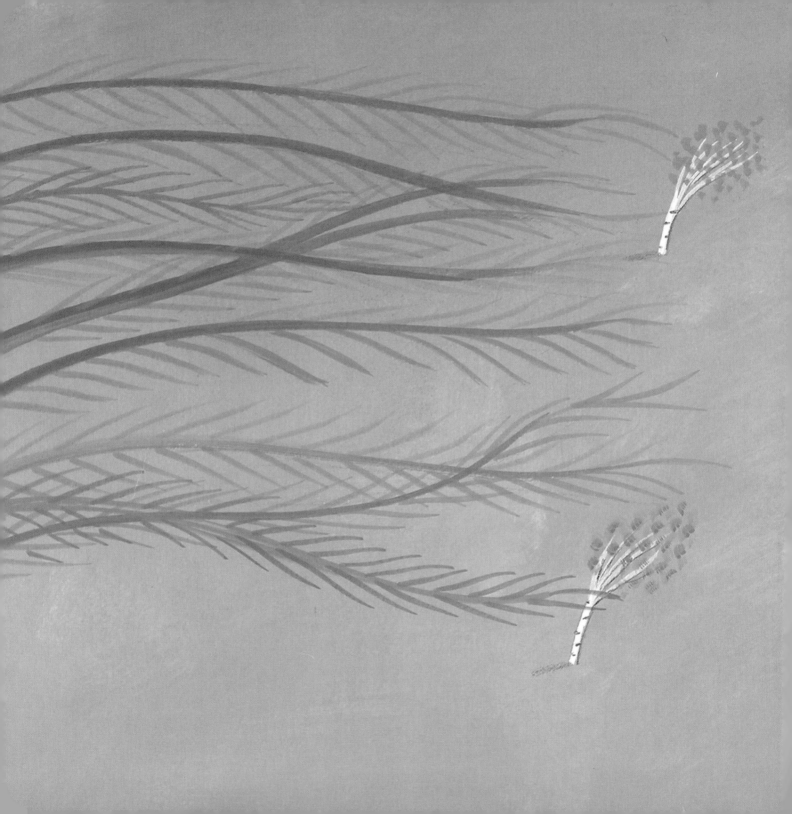

tolled a bell
atop a church

chased some crows

flung them far

*strummed on a
telephone wire guitar*

thrumming a tune
mile on mile
all the while you were

chasing